Captain McGrew Wants

YOU
for his Crew!

Mark Sperring   **Ed Eaves**

BLOOMSBURY

LONDON OXFORD NEW YORK NEW DELHI SYDNEY

Meet Captain McGrew:
He's in need of a crew
to do all those jobs
that pirate crews do.

You'll need bulging muscles
(strong fingers, strong thumbs)
to HOIST up the main sail
and wave . . .

GOODBYE, MUM!

You **HAVE** to be tough,
that has to be said,
to **PULL** up the anchor
from the sea bed . . .

You mustn't be little
and you mustn't be BIG,

but just the right size to

GET UP
THAT RIG!

You MUST be prepared to SHOUT:

LAND AHOY!

And go by the title of

LAD,

LASS

or BOY!

Are you good with a spade?

Do you complain if you're HOT?

Can you dig for **LONG** hours while others . . .

CANNOT?

And while Captain McGrew
sits in the cool shade,
can you make him a snack
and **SQUEEZE** lemonade?

Can you H-EE-EE-AVE out the treasure all by YOURSELF?

Can you SPLOOSH down the POOP DECK?

BATTEN the HATCH?

And though you're plum tired, YES, after all THAT,
could you go to the galley and heat up a vat?

Then RUSTLE up supper
for Captain McGrew.
Something so simple . . .

like OCTOPUS STEW?

Would you **DO THE DISHES** with no word of thanks?

Or grab hold of a broom and start **WALKING THE PLANK?**

Could you clean off the hull,
till it's tidy and neat?

And NEVER,

NO NEVER,

find time for a sleep?

Can you read bedtime stories?

Sing sweet songs you know?

Navigate through the night
as McGrew snores below?

I hope you CAN do this,
YES, REALLY, I do,
for I know a pirate who's
picked out his crew . . .

And
SHIVER-ME-TIMBERS
(uh-oh)
IT'S YOU!
YES, Captain McGrew
wants YOU
for his crew!

But for those who **AREN'T** suited
to a life on the waves . . .

there's a knight here
called **Norman**
who's been looking
for knaves!

HELP WANTED